THE Fr... V...ng...

The Reindeer and the Snowy Owl

Written and illustrated by

Marisa Peña

SNOWDROP
BOOKS

A Fairy World Book

Redmond, Washington

SNOWY MEADOWS

Cloud Top
Mountain

Snowy Owl
Village

Snow Haven

Cascade
Range

Springtime Sea

Mossy Vale

Feather
Cliffs

Fox Tail
Hollow

Hoof Print
Glade

Puffin Beak

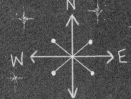

THE FROST WINGS

Charm Iceglade - *Maker*
Charm has The Power of Magical
Sewing. She can use it to create
magical items.

Lucy Dawn - *Healer*
Lucy has magical healing abilities. She
also loves to learn about the plants and
animals of the Arctic.

Willow Brightfrost - *Spellcaster*
Willow has a magic wand. She can cast
a variety of spells for fire, ice, wind,
water, and earth.

North Everstar - *Navigator*
North has a magical bow and arrow.
She has very sharp eyesight and
powerful hearing.

This book is dedicated to the Arctic.

www.snowdropbooks.com

Printed in the United States of America

Written and illustrated by Marisa Peña

Cover design by Jenny Rez

Cover art by Marisa Peña

Names: Peña, Marisa L., author.

Title: The frost wings : the reindeer and the snowy owl / written and illustrated by Marisa Peña.

Series: The Frost Wings

Description: Redmond, WA: Snowdrop Books, 2024. | Summary: Willow, North, Charm, and Lucy continue their adventures as Frost Wings, helping new animal friends and developing their magical powers.

Identifiers: LCCN: 2023915868| ISBN: 978-1-960834-05-8 (hardcover) | 978-1-960834-04-1 (paperback) | 978-1-960834-06-5 (ebook) | 978-1-960834-07-2 (audio)

Subjects: LCSH: Fairies--Juvenile fiction. | Reindeer--Juvenile fiction. | Snowy owl--Juvenile fiction. | Arctic animals--Juvenile fiction. | Fantasy fiction. | BISAC JUVENILE FICTION / Fantasy & Magic | JUVENILE FICTION / Action & Adventure / General | JUVENILE FICTION / Animals / General | JUVENILE FICTION / Places / Polar Regions | JUVENILE FICTION / Readers / Chapter Books

Classification: LCC PZ7.1 .P46 Fr 2024 | DDC [Fic]--dc23

TABLE OF CONTENTS

CHAPTER 1
ALMOST WINTER

It was a clear and cold day in the Arctic. Winter was coming. The land was buried in fluffy snow and shimmering ice.

The sun was low on the horizon. In the winter, there are only a few hours of twilight before it is dark again.

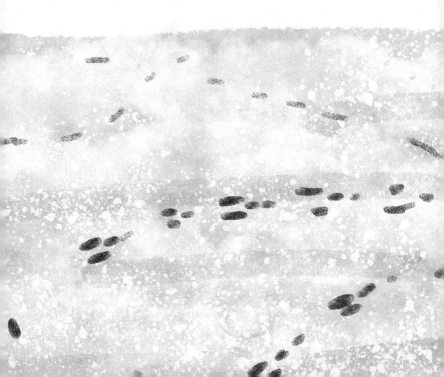

Lucy was inside Snow Haven, the fairy home she shared with the Frost Wings in the land of Snowy Meadows.

She was sitting in a soft chair made of twisted willow twigs. She was staying warm under a blanket of musk ox wool.

She was reading by the light of a star lamp, enchanted with fairy magic. It gave off a soft bright glow.

Her book was called *Everything About Lemmings*. She was excited to learn about these small rodents. They were one of the few animals to stay active through the Arctic winter. Most other animals left for warmer places, or they hibernated.

Willow and North were playing outside with twelve Arctic hares. They were in two teams, playing a game of Don't Step on the Track.

The Arctic hares tried to hop across the field without stepping on any tracks already in the snow. If they stepped on a track, they were out.

The winning team was the one that could get more hares to the other side successfully.

North and Willow were the game referees. They each rode on the backs of the hares, calling out any hopper that stepped on a track.

Charm was in a nearby field. She could hear all the laughter. And she could hear all the arguments!

"You're out, Fluff Foot!" called North. She thrust her thumb out.

"Hey, I only touched the track with my toe!" Fluff Foot protested.

"Even a toe counts, Fluff Foot," North said firmly.

Charm was digging holes in the snow in that nearby field. She wanted to make the most of the few hours of daylight she had today.

She was cold and exhausted. But she did not want to take a break.

CHAPTER 2
THE MAGIC ROPE

Charm was searching for rare plants
hidden under the snow. She needed
them to make a new Magic Thread.

At the Autumn Celebration ceremony,
the Arctic Fairy Queen gave Charm
a Magic Thread. It shimmered with
rainbow colors in the light. It would
bring magic to whatever item Charm
sewed it into.

To replace her Magic Thread, Charm
would need to weave a new one. She
was taught the process by the Arctic
Fairy Queen, in a rhyme. Charm learned
it by heart.

Rainbow moss, shimmering bright.
Rainbow lichen, so rarely in sight.
A feather from a snowy owl.
Master of flight.
With the heart must be given.
Never asked for or taken.
Woven together,
Under the Northern Lights.

Charm had used her Magic Thread to make a magic rope. But Blaze took it when they were helping a young Arctic fox get home. Ever since Blaze took that rope, Charm could not stop searching for the ingredients she needed to make a new thread.

It wasn't much use to search in the winter when everything was buried in snow. But her heart was restless. Searching for ingredients was the only thing that made her feel better.

Her daydreams were interrupted
when she heard Lucy calling her name.
"Charm! The queen is calling!"

CHAPTER 3
MESSAGE FROM THE QUEEN

Charm flew back with Lucy. The Frost
Wings gathered around the twinkling
wind chimes outside their home. A
ribbon of enchanted and glittering air
surrounded them. It carried the voice
of the Arctic Fairy Queen.

"Hello, Frost Wings," greeted the queen. "This morning, I sensed an unusual presence of our fairy magic. I think it may be coming from the magic rope that Blaze stole from Charm. This likely points the way to Blaze's camp."

Charm's heart leaped. They might know where her rope is! But her excitement was also mixed with fear.

Blaze and her minions were a frightening sight. She didn't like the idea of encountering them, much less on Blaze's home turf. Still, she felt an urgent pull toward Blaze. She wanted to get her magic rope back.

The queen sensed Charm's feelings. "Charm, I know you are eager to get your rope back. I do not want to put you in harm's way. But I fear that Blaze will use the rope for her awful purposes. So, I trust you to be careful while you investigate Blaze's camp. Most importantly, do not get hurt."

"Thank you, Your Highness. I understand," said Charm.

Then they said goodbye. The fairies gathered their things. They were going to Blaze's camp.

CHAPTER 4
ALFRED

The fairies flew toward the location of Blaze's camp. North, the Frost Wings Navigator, led the way.

By the time they arrived, the sun had set. The sky was filled with brilliant stars. The moon was full and bright. The light of the full moon shone on a grim looking camp below.

The fairies landed behind a large boulder, just out of sight. They peered around the boulder to get a better look at the camp.

They could see the details of the fence in front. It was made of gnarled, thorny branches. The branches twisted together to make the shapes of letters: B L A Z E.

"I think we can safely say we found Blaze's camp," said North.

Then they heard a voice calling through the darkness. "Henry! Oh Henry! Are you out here?!"

A lemming came into view.

When he spotted the fairies, he waved and called over to them. "Oh wow, fairies! Hello!"

He counted them as if he were counting berries on a bush, pointing at each one. "One. Two. Three. Four. You must be the Frost Wings! Word has gotten around about you. Lemmings have a mighty fine network of communication, if I do say so myself."

And before the fairies could say so much as a greeting, he continued. "I am wondering, have you seen another lemming around here that looks like me? Short legs, small ears, two long teeth in front."

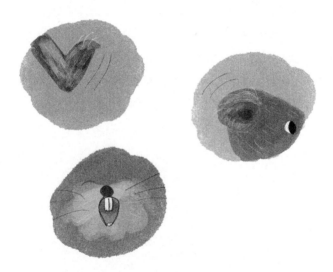

With each mention of a body part, he pointed or tugged on his own, calling attention to it.

"He goes by the name of Henry. He is my brother. I, myself, am Alfred. Henry has been missing since yesterday," he said.

"No, we haven't," replied Lucy. "We just arrived. We came with a plan to go in there," she said with a frown. She pointed solemnly toward the thorny gates.

Alfred looked over, and his face dropped. "Oh my. I see. A rather grim looking place. Oh my. Do you think Henry could be in there?" he said with a new shakiness in his voice.

CHAPTER 5
THE TUNNELS

"It's possible," replied Lucy gently, not wanting to alarm Alfred. "We hope to find a way to get in there. But we need to get in without a certain fairy named Blaze seeing us."

"Oh yes, I see. I see that someone named Blaze must live here," Alfred said as he looked up at the big sign.

And then after a pause, Alfred's face brightened with an idea. "Oh, now just a minute. Just a minute. My goodness. I think I have a fine idea. Oh yes, I do! We lemmings have a mighty fine system of tunnels under the snow, if I do say so myself. We could use our tunnels to go into the camp unseen."

"That would be great!" North exclaimed. North loved exploring tunnels. The other three fairies were a little less enthusiastic.

The fairies followed Alfred to an opening by a large boulder. They followed him down the tunnel.

Once the fairies got inside, they were delightfully surprised. "These tunnels are amazing!" declared Lucy.

They stretched on and on,
branching off in countless different
directions. And there were different
rooms for different purposes.

Alfred proudly showed them
around. "Here are the nests. This is
where we sleep. And here is where we
store food."

The food storage rooms were carefully organized. There were neat groups of frozen plants, moss shoots, bark, and twigs.

The nesting rooms were especially beautiful. They were lined with all kinds of moss and lichen.

Charm gushed, "Oh wow, Alfred! These nesting sites are so beautiful! The colors! The textures!"

"Oh yes, yes," he replied. "This is all the work of my brother, Henry. A real artist, he is. He is always out searching for beautiful materials to decorate with. Sometimes, I worry that he will bring in so much that there will be no room to sleep!"

Charm felt a special connection to Henry. She was the Frost Wings Maker. She loved making things too.

After traveling through another long series of tunnels, Alfred stopped in front of one. "This one opens to the ground," he said. "If we go through this opening, we'll arrive on the other side of Blaze's fence."

"Thank you, Alfred," replied North. "I'll go first and just pop my head up. I'll tell you what I see."

North had an exceptionally good sense of sight. She could see things others could not. She put her head through the opening and looked over at the camp.

Once she saw what was going on, she felt a huge lump of concern and sadness in her throat. She no longer wanted to tell them what she saw.

CHAPTER 6
SOUNDS IN THE DARK

North first noticed a red crow standing guard out front. She recognized this bird! It was Blaze's enchanted crow. It had red feathers and red eyes.

Six fairy minions stood guard as well. They had the same red wings and red eyes as the crow. They stared blankly ahead, as if in a trance.

There were more minions than they had ever seen. Blaze's crew was growing bigger!

Then North looked closely at the shelter that the minions were guarding. The shelter was made of animal bones. North could see Blaze inside.

Blaze was reclining in a chair. Steam rose from the hot drink she held.

Beside her, there was a lemming lifted high off the ground, suspended by a rope. Charm's rope!

The lemming was chiseling the face of a large ice sculpture. It was in the form of Blaze, standing with arms bent at her hips.

Blaze called up from her chair, over to the lemming. "Make sure you capture the essence of my high cheek bones, Lemming! They are one of my finest features. Do a good job and I won't make you haul the biggest bones tomorrow."

North went back down the hole to describe the situation to the team. "The good news is that the rope is there," she said. "The bad news is that it is being used to trap a lemming. Alfred, I think it may be Henry."

Alfred gasped. "Oh my. Oh my. What will we do?!"

"Do not worry, Alfred," Willow replied. "We'll think of something. We will get him home."

"There are six fairy minions standing guard, along with Blaze's crow," North continued.

Then Willow had an idea.

"North, what if you used your Animal Sounds Arrow to create a distraction? This might get Blaze and her minions away from camp. Then we can go in to free Henry."

North and the other fairies liked this plan, and they agreed to try it.

North loaded the arrow into her bow and pulled it back. She said the magic words.

An angry polar bear
Is what we need to hear.
Make this frightening sound
For everyone to fear.

The arrow flew into the darkness. It exploded into a series of booming, growling sounds that sounded like an angry polar bear.

Blaze sat up straight in alarm. "What was that terrible noise?! A polar bear? Minions, investigate!"

The minions flew in the direction of the sound. They disappeared into the darkness of the night as they followed the rumbling growls.

North kept shooting new arrows into the sky, drawing the minions further away from camp.

"It worked!" Willow cried. "The minions are gone!"

"But unfortunately, Blaze didn't leave," added North.

"Hmmm. We need a way to scare her off," thought Lucy out loud.

CHAPTER 7
A FEARSOME SHADOW

"I have an idea!" exclaimed Lucy.

"Alfred, do you think you can
create a scary shadow with your body?"
Lucy asked.

Alfred puffed up his chest and was
quite pleased by this idea. "Why I
am a rather good actor, if I do say so
myself. Just last summer, I performed
the great Duke of Lemmingshire in our
community play."

"Great!" Lucy replied. "Willow, will
you use your wand to create a bright
light? You can cast a big shadow of
Alfred to scare Blaze away."

"Great idea!" exclaimed Willow. "Let's go!" Willow ushered Alfred off to his new stage.

"Okay, Alfred. Stand right here and strike your scariest pose!" Willow instructed. "I will light you from behind."

"Oh yes, I will pretend I am the fearsome Count Lemming of Ice Grove!" Alfred said.

Alfred stood on his hind legs. He lifted his front limbs in a most threatening pose. He held out his paws. He stuck out his claws. He made the scariest face he could!

Willow waved her magic wand and said the magic words.

Luminous glow, bright light.
Cast a beam into the night!

The light shone from her wand and lit Alfred from behind. A huge frightening shadow fell over Blaze.

"Ahh!!" Blaze cried. She jumped out of her seat, dropped her cup, and ran! "Eat the lemming! He's meatier!"

She darted to the crow. She jumped on his back. "Fly, Crow, fly!"

Charm and Lucy ran over to the
lemming that was suspended by the
rope. "Is that you, Henry?" they asked.

"Yes, it is! I am Henry," he replied.
"Are you here to help me?"

"Yes, we are!" Charm exclaimed.

The fairies untied the rope and
lowered Henry to the ground. Then
they freed him from the rope harness.

"We better run! Blaze might come
back!" urged Lucy.

CHAPTER 8
MARGARET

Sure enough, Lucy and Charm could see the crow returning in the sky.

Lucy, Charm, and Henry ran! Charm took one last look at the rope. She was tempted to take the extra time to free it from the wooden beam. But she knew it was too risky.

She felt a pang in her heart as she ran. She tried to console herself. *Maybe tomorrow*, she thought.

The fairies and Henry ran to Alfred. The lemming brothers were joyfully reunited. They hugged one another for a long time.

Then Alfred led the way back through the tunnels and to their nesting sites.

When they arrived, there was a hubbub among the lemmings. They were gathered in a large group.

"What is it, Peter?" asked Alfred.

A young lemming explained. "There is a reindeer outside the Old Birch entrance. She did not migrate with the rest of the herd. She seems to have forgotten how to get to her usual winter grounds."

"We have been many places in Snowy Meadows. We might be able to help," Willow suggested.

The fairies and the lemmings went outside to talk to the reindeer.

Willow introduced herself. "Hello, Reindeer! My name is Willow, of the Frost Wings. How are you?"

"Oh hello, Dear. Can you fly a little closer so I can get a good look at you?" replied the reindeer.

"Of course!" Willow flew closer to her eyes.

"Oh, now aren't you lovely?" she said. "My name is Margaret. It is nice to meet you."

"It is nice to meet you, Margaret. I have heard that you are no longer with your herd. Do you know where they were headed?" Willow asked.

"Oh yes, Dear. I don't remember what happened exactly. Hmmm... let me think." And then after a long pause, she continued.

"I have four sons, three daughters, and fourteen grandchildren. Can you believe that? Oh yes, Moondance is the newest one. Oh, he is so cute. Wait a moment. You asked me a question, Dear?" Margaret said.

"Yes, we are wondering if you remember where you are going for the winter," replied Willow.

"Oh, that's right. I don't remember how to get there exactly. Or maybe it's better to say, I keep forgetting. I walk in the wrong direction and get confused. My memory isn't as good as it used to be. I do remember that it's near a mountain in the shape of a puffin's beak," Margaret replied.

"I know where that is," said North. "Puffin Beak Mountain. And I know how to get there!"

"And we can all go with you," offered Willow.

"You would go with me?" said
Margaret with surprise. "Oh my, it
would be such a wonderful thing to
have such companions!"

"We would be delighted,"
responded the fairies. They all agreed
that they would leave in the morning.

Charm was happy to accompany
Margaret. But she knew it meant giving
up her plan to go back to Blaze's camp
in the morning. It was painful to walk
away from another chance to get her
rope back. But going with Margaret
was the right thing to do. There was no
time to lose. Winter was coming fast.

CHAPTER 9
THE GIFT

That night, Margaret laid down to sleep behind a large boulder, away from the night wind. The fairies slept in the lovely nesting rooms.

In the morning, Alfred woke them up. He served them a nice breakfast of frozen berry smoothies.

"It's a wonderfully delicious recipe, if I do say so myself," he said.

And he was right! They were so delicious. The fairies enjoyed their breakfast immensely.

Outside, the fairies began to say goodbye to their new lemming friends.

Henry told them to wait an extra moment. He had something for them.

Henry disappeared down a tunnel. He returned with a wrapped gift. It was tied with a beautiful ribbon made of dried grass. He gave it to Charm.

"I would like to give this gift to you and your friends. I thought you might like it for your own home. It is one of the most beautiful things I have ever found on the tundra," he said.

Charm opened the gift. She couldn't believe her eyes. It was a tuft of multi-colored moss. It glimmered in the sunlight. She remembered the words to the rhyme.

Rainbow moss, shimmering bright.

It was like nothing she had ever seen. Charm was speechless. "I simply can't tell you how much this means to me. Thank you, Henry!"

"I hope you all have a good and safe journey," Henry said. "Please come back to see us someday."

"We will!" said the fairies.

They departed. North led the way to Puffin Beak Mountain.

CHAPTER 10
THADDEUS

As they walked, they made frequent stops for Margaret to eat. She dug the snow with her hoof to uncover lichen.

During one of their meal breaks, a snowy owl was perched on a rock nearby, also poking around for food.

Upon seeing the reindeer, he introduced himself. "Hello, my name is Thaddeus. I see you have chosen to stay through the winter. Most of the reindeer have traveled to the edge of the tundra to find more food."

"Hello, Thaddeus. My name is Margaret. It is nice to meet you. I did not mean to stay behind. I somehow got separated from my herd," replied Margaret. "These lovely fairies are traveling with me to Puffin Beak Mountain. I will rejoin my herd there."

"Oh, splendid!" said Thaddeus. "That is quite the coincidence. I am heading there myself. I should have departed weeks ago."

"I was working on my lectures on *The Myths of The Great Snowy Owl*," he continued. "I simply lost track of time. I often lose track of time when studying these majestic stories."

"That is wonderful," Margaret responded. "I love the stories of The Great Snowy Owl."

"Yes, me too," Willow said. "My mother told me those stories when I was young. Would you like to join us to Puffin Beak Mountain, Thaddeus?"

"It would be my pleasure. Thank you," Thaddeus replied.

The fairies were delighted to have a new travel companion on their journey.

And so, the team continued onwards. As they traveled, Margaret made frequent stops to dig in the snow with her hooves to find lichen to eat. And Thaddeus told stories about The Great Snowy Owl to pass the time.

Neither Margaret nor the owl seemed to be in much of a hurry. One had a lot of eating to do. And the other had a lot of stories to tell. The days passed. Eat. Walk. Eat. Sleep. Eat some more.

But then the weather turned.

The wind and snow blew fiercely. Thaddeus perched on Margaret's back, and the fairies flew under her belly as a shield from the wind.

"Do you hear that?" Lucy called over the howling wind. "It's the clicking sound of Margaret's ankles. Reindeer use this sound to stay together when they can't see in a snowstorm. We can follow that sound to stay close to each other!"

After a while, they stopped so that North could get a better look at what was ahead.

Through the snow, she spotted the outline of Puffin Beak Mountain in the distance. "I think we are getting close!" she yelled to the others over the howling wind.

CHAPTER 11
LOST IN THE SNOW

"We just need to get through this mountain pass." North continued. "We should get there by morning."

Thaddeus wanted to get a better view of Puffin Beak Mountain. He flew to a higher spot on the cliffside and landed on a snowy boulder.

Just then, there was a loud rumble.
The boulder shifted with the moving
snow. There was a large *CRACK*
followed by a thundering *ROAR*. Snow
tumbled down the mountain, carrying
Thaddeus with it.

Everything moved so quickly, the
fairies could not see where he went.

North immediately shot an arrow into the sky and called out.

To Thaddeus' side
Is where we must be.
Show us a trail
By land, air, or sea!

A glittering, purple trail stretched across the snowfield.

North called to the others. "Let's hurry! Follow the trail!"

Margaret went into a full gallop. They did not know she could run so fast! The fairies flew alongside her.

CHAPTER 12
STRONG ANTLERS

The fairies and Margaret arrived to see Thaddeus lying on his side in the snow.

The fairies rushed over to him. "Thaddeus are you okay?!" they cried.

Margaret slowly walked up to Thaddeus. She bent her head down and brought her head close to his. "How are you doing, Dear?" she said gently.

"Oh, that was quite a spill," responded Thaddeus with a touch of strain to his voice. "It reminds me of tumbling about in the snow when I was a small owlet. But I'm not quite as limber as I used to be. I broke my wing, I'm afraid."

"Oh yes, we do get old, don't we," Margaret said. She carefully and tenderly scooped Thaddeus into her antlers. "Now I believe you were in the middle of a story. *The Great Snowy Owl flew into the howling winds ...*"

"Oh yes, that's right," said Thaddeus. "The Great Snowy Owl flew into the howling winds. His mighty wings beat against the sky ..."

Margaret stood still as she listened to the story. She held Thaddeus in the cradle of her antlers, waiting for North to lead the way through the blizzard.

But North knew that it was too dangerous to travel any further. "The wind is too strong," she cautioned. "It will freeze us soon if we don't find some shelter."

CHAPTER 13
THE GREAT SNOWY OWL

The friends stood there in the rapidly dropping temperature.

"This is only going to get worse once the sun goes down," said Willow. "We don't have much time left."

"I would like to tell you a story that I think will help," said Thaddeus.

"In *The Great Snowy Owl and the Menace*, there is a terrible blizzard," he said. "The Great Snowy Owl is leading a legion of animals. They are at great risk of freezing to death! So, The Great Snowy Owl begins digging enormous trenches with his talons. He commands everyone to get inside. Inside the trenches, they are protected from the winds."

"Ah, then we should dig," said Margaret, understanding Thaddeus perfectly.

Margaret began digging a trench with her hooves. Willow used her wind spell to help. She pointed her wand to the snow and said the magic words.

A wind so strong, a wind so fast.
Time to blow, time to blast!

Blasts of air exploded into the snow, expanding the trench Margaret was digging with her hooves.

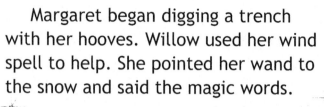

Once the trench was big enough, Margaret laid down in it. She carefully placed Thaddeus down into a protected corner. The fairies nestled beside her warm fur. The wind and snow blew overhead.

Lucy went to Thaddeus. "Thaddeus, I have some healing magic that I can use to help you."

"That would be splendid," said Thaddeus softly. He was just starting to fall asleep. He was exhausted from the events of the day.

Lucy borrowed an arrow
from North. It was made
of strong wood.

She tore off the hem
of her dress to make a
bandage.

She held the broken wing bones
together to make one bone again. Then
she placed the arrow against the bone.
She tied the bandage around it to hold
the broken bones together.

Then she began to rub her hands. Golden sparkles jumped from them.

The more she rubbed her hands, the more sparkles appeared. Soon, Thaddeus was showered with golden, sparkling light.

She sang her healing song, and the sound of the howling wind seemed to fade away.

May your heart be comforted
From injuries that take their toll.
May a healing warmth embrace you
And make your broken parts whole.

Thaddeus was nearly asleep. But he stayed awake just long enough to hear the song. He found Lucy's voice so beautiful and soothing. He remembered being a young owlet so many years ago, being sung to by his grandmother. He drifted off to sleep.

As Margaret also dozed off, the fairies agreed they would stay awake through the night to keep watch. It was the strongest blizzard they had ever seen.

Willow created a warm glow with her magic wand. The fairies huddled around it to stay warm through the freezing night.

CHAPTER 14
MIGHTY HOOVES

By morning, the blizzard had passed. The wind had blown the storm clouds away. The sky was clear.

When Thaddeus awoke, he flapped his wings. "My goodness! I can move my wing! Look here, Margaret!" he said, as he flapped his wing up and down.

"Oh, that is marvelous, Thaddeus," said Margaret.

Thaddeus took flight. He swooped around in the air simply to enjoy the feeling of flight again.

"I am going to look around for a bit of breakfast," Margaret said to the fairies.

She walked to a clearing. She hoofed the snow, digging for hidden lichen underneath. As she dug at the snow, a twinkle on the ground caught Charm's eye.

Charm flew closer to see what was twinkling in the snow.

There in front of her, just beside Margaret's hoof, was the most beautiful patch of rainbow lichen Charm had ever seen! It was the kind of lichen she had dreamed of finding ever since Blaze took her magic rope.

"Margaret, you did it!" exclaimed Charm.

"What did I do, Dear?" asked Margaret.

"You helped me find a rare lichen I have been searching for! I wasn't sure I would ever find it!" exclaimed Charm.

"Oh my, that's just wonderful, Dear," Margaret said. "Would you like me to hoof some more?"

Charm cried with delight. "Yes, please do, Margaret!"

Margaret exposed more of the lichen by digging with her hooves.

Charm dove down. She gathered a bunch into her arms. The lichen twinkled. It glittered. It danced in the sunlight.

Rainbow lichen, so rarely in sight.

76

CHAPTER 15
A MAGICAL NIGHT

The team continued through the mountain pass. That afternoon, they arrived at a large clearing. They could see reindeer tracks everywhere.

"There, look! Puffin Beak Mountain!" called North, pointing toward the mountain.

Yes, everyone could see it! The mountain certainly looked like a puffin's beak! They all cheered.

Thaddeus took this moment to express the gratitude he felt.

"Fairies. Margaret. I want to thank you for this amazing journey," he said. "Your fairy magic healed my wing, and your wonderful company filled my heart."

"I wish to present a feather to each of you," he continued. "It is something to remind you of our time together."

Thaddeus plucked five of his feathers and held them in his beak. He flew to each fairy, dropping a feather at each of their feet. He gave Willow a second one. He asked her if she would kindly present it to Margaret.

Willow tucked the feather behind Margaret's ear. It made Margaret smile. "You look lovely," said Willow.

Charm was trembling with joy. She couldn't believe her eyes. She held the gift in her arms. Tears of gratitude filled her eyes.

A feather from a snowy owl.
Master of flight.
With the heart must be given.
Never asked for or taken.

Just then, a young reindeer
emerged from beyond a snowy
hill. Another voice could be heard.
"Moondance! Not too far!"

"Did they just say, Moondance?"
asked Willow. "Wasn't that the name
of Margaret's grandson?"

As Moondance got closer to them,
he called out. "Grandma!"

Margaret moved her head forward.
"I know that voice! That's my little
Moondance! Come closer, Darling, so I
can see you better!" she said.

Moondance ran toward Margaret
and nuzzled his head into her legs.
"Oh, my goodness, this is just
wonderful!" Margaret cheered.

An older deer came forward. "Mom! You made it!" he said. "We were worried about you. We thought you were with George, and he thought you were with us. A terrible mistake. We didn't realize it until we arrived at Puffin Beak Mountain," he explained. "We are so sorry."

"Oh, it was no trouble at all, Dear," she replied. "I made some new friends. Meet the fairies, North, Lucy, Willow, and Charm. And meet Thaddeus. He is a wonderful storyteller."

"It is so good to meet all of you," said the reindeer. "Thank you for joining my mother on her journey home. We hope you will spend the evening with us."

"It would be my pleasure," said Thaddeus. The fairies agreed.

They followed the reindeer to where the herd was resting and eating.

Everyone settled in for the evening. They gathered around Thaddeus who perched on a rock and told stories into the night.

And in that clear dark night, stars filled the sky. Glowing ribbons of pink and green light began dancing in the sky. Swirling and shining, the Northern Lights were a symphony of color.

Out in the snowfield, under the dancing Northern Lights, Charm set out her treasures.

Rainbow moss. A gift from a lemming artist named Henry.

Rainbow lichen. A treasure found under Margaret's mighty reindeer hooves.

A snowy owl feather. A gift from Thaddeus, a masterful storyteller.

She began to weave a Magic Thread.
Rainbow moss, shimmering bright.
Rainbow lichen, so rarely in sight.
A feather from a snowy owl.
Master of flight.
With the heart must be given.
Never asked for or taken.
Woven together,
Under the Northern Lights.

I know exactly what I'm going to make this time, she thought.

Read the Next
Frost Wings Adventure!

The Frost Wings: Baby Harp Seals at the Springtime Sea

What will Charm make with her Magic Thread?

What surprising discovery do the Frost Wings make about Blaze?

Will they be able to help a baby harp seal in need?

LUCY'S ANIMAL NOTES

Lemmings

❄ Lemmings do not hibernate. They remain active all winter.

❄ They eat grass, moss, berries, shoots, and roots.

❄ They have burrow systems with special rooms. They have food storage rooms and nesting rooms.

❄ Their teeth never stop growing. They chew on tough foods to file them down.

Reindeer

❄ Reindeer are the only deer species where the females have antlers.

❄ They are the only deer species with hair that covers their noses.

❄ They eat mosses, herbs, ferns, and grasses. They also eat the shoots and leaves of shrubs and trees, especially willow and birch.

❄ In the winter, they mainly eat lichen when other food is not available.

Snowy Owl

* Snowy owl have feet covered with feathers, like fluffy slippers.

* They can hunt in the daylight. This is useful in the Arctic, where the sun does not set all summer long.

* Male snowy owls are almost completely white.

* Female snowy owls have dark brown stripes on their white feathers.

THE FROST WINGS SERIES

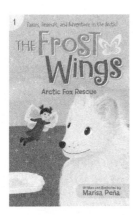

THANK YOU

Dear Reader,

Thank you for reading the second Frost Wings adventure! I hope you enjoyed it.

If you liked this book, please leave a review on Amazon.com. I would love to hear what you think!

Thank you!
- Marisa

ABOUT THE AUTHOR

Marisa Peña lives in Washington state with her husband, two children, and a very sweet kitty cat named Mochi.

Along with writing and drawing, she loves spending time with her family, growing food, and running on trails in the woods.

Marisa is also a board game inventor. She has co-invented dozens of award-winning board games for kids and families, including *Outfoxed!*, *Dinosaur Escape*, and *The Fairy Game*. You can see all her games at: www.departmentofrec.com.

Printed in Great Britain
by Amazon